A NORTH-SOUTH PAPERBACK

Critical praise for

Grandpa's Amazing Computer

"A boy visits his grandfather and they have a chat about computers, but that's not all that happens in a tale that succeeds on several levels. . . . The story highlights the boy's first independent trip on the train, and also explores a potential rift in his relationship with the older man; Ollie is unwittingly smug about his high-tech proclivities, but Grandpa knows how to smooth the way."

Kirkus

Grandpa's Amazing Computer

By Ursel Scheffler

Illustrated by
Ruth Scholte van Mast

Translated by Rosemary Lanning

North-South Books

NEW YORK / LONDON

/ / DEC 2008

Copyright © 1997 by Nord-Süd Verlag AG, Gossau Zürich, Switzerland
First published in Switzerland under the title *Opas Computer-Geheimnis*.
English translation copyright © 1997 by North-South Books Inc.

First published in the United States, Great Britain, Canada,
Australia, and New Zealand in 1997 by North-South Books,
an imprint of Nord-Süd Verlag AG, Gossau Zürich, Switzerland.
First published in paperback in 1999.

Distributed in the United States by North-South Books Inc., New York.

Library of Congress Cataloging-in-Publication Data
Scheffler, Ursel.
[Opas Computer-Geheimnis. English]
Grandpa's amazing computer / by Ursel Scheffler ; illustrated by
Ruth Scholte van Mast ; translated by Rosemary Lanning.
Summary: Thinking that his grandfather doesn't know anything about computers,
ten-year-old Ollie is amazed when the old gentleman claims to have one of the
world's oldest ones lying around somewhere.
[1. Grandfathers—Fiction. 2. Computers—Fiction.]
I. Scholte van Mast, Ruth, ill. II. Lanning, Rosemary. III. Title.
PZ7.S3425Gr 1997
[E]—dc21 97-13657

A CIP catalogue record for this book
is available from The British Library.

ISBN 1-55858-795-0 (TRADE BINDING)
1 3 5 7 9 TB 10 8 6 4 2
ISBN 1-55858-796-9 (LIBRARY BINDING)
1 3 5 7 9 LB 10 8 6 4 2
ISBN 0-7358-1100-8 (PAPERBACK)
1 3 5 7 9 PB 10 8 6 4 2
Printed in Belgium

For more information about our books, and the authors and artists
who create them, visit our web site: http://www.northsouth.com

On his way home from school one day,
Ollie met the postman, who handed him
a letter.

"It's from Grandpa," said Ollie, looking
pleased.

Ollie ran all the way home.

He rushed into the kitchen, startling his mother. She nearly dropped the spaghetti she was cooking.

"Grandpa has written me a letter," Ollie told her. "Shall I read it to you?"

"Yes, please," she said.

Ollie read:

> *Dear Ollie,*
>
> *It was very nice to get your letter.*
>
> *It would be even nicer if you could come and visit me.*
>
> *Would you like to come next weekend?*
>
> *Love from*
> *Grandpa*

Ollie's mother looked at the calendar.
"Next weekend would be good," she said.
"If you're with Grandpa, I can go to the
computer show with Dad. But," she added,
looking doubtful, "you would have to
travel on your own."

"I'll be fine," said Ollie. "I'm nearly ten,
remember?"

As soon as he had finished eating, Ollie
went up to his room and wrote a letter to
Grandpa.

> Dear Grandpa,
> I can come! Next weekend Mother and
> Father are going to a computer show.
> They say I can travel on my own.
> See you on Saturday.
>   Love from
>   Ollie

On Saturday
morning Ollie was
on the train to Grandpa's.

Dad had written out a list of
stations for him. Grandpa's was the
seventh. When the ticket collector
came to check Ollie's ticket, he said,
"You want to get off at the next stop."

"I know," said Ollie. "The next station
is Forest Hills. That's where my grandpa
lives."

The train was a quarter of an hour late. Grandpa was starting to get anxious.

The longer he waited, the more he worried that Ollie might have got off at the wrong station.

At last the train came around the bend.

It stopped with a squeal of brakes. A door flew open, and Ollie jumped out.

"Grandpa!" called Ollie. He ran up and hugged his grandfather. Then Ollie looked over Grandpa's shoulder and saw a small dog. "Who's that?" he asked.

"It's Mr. Major," said Grandpa. "I thought you would like to meet him. I'm looking after him while my friend is in the hospital."

"That's good," said Ollie. He liked dogs. "Can I take his leash?" he asked.

"Of course you can. But let me take your bag."

Mr. Major tugged at his leash all the way to Grandpa's.

Ollie had to hold on tight.

"Grandpa, do you remember that story you told me last year? The one about the man with the magic dog?"

Grandpa shook his head. "No. Can't say I remember that one," he said.

"You can't have forgotten the whole story!" said Ollie.

Grandpa sighed. "I'm afraid my memory isn't as good as it used to be."

"You need a computer," Ollie said. "They have lots of memory."

"A computer? What would I do with one of them?" said Grandpa. He sounded horrified.

"Dad has one," said Ollie. "He records everything on it—numbers and other important things. Then, if he forgets something, he looks it up on the computer."

"I see," said Grandpa doubtfully.

"Dad says he couldn't manage without his computer."

"Your father has to like computers," muttered Grandpa. "He sells the things."

"Here we are," said Grandpa. "You
can let Mr. Major off the leash now."
The dog scampered upstairs.
"I think he's hungry," said Grandpa.
As they climbed the stairs, Ollie sniffed.
"What's that funny smell?" he asked.

"My cake!" gasped Grandpa. "I forgot to turn the oven off!"

Grandpa rushed into the kitchen and took the cake out of the oven. "Well, it could be worse," he said. "It's only slightly burned. Let's pretend it's a chocolate cake."

"You need a computerized oven, like the one we have at home," Ollie said. "It switches itself off when the cake is done."

"You and your computers," said Grandpa. He sounded irritated.

At lunch Ollie asked, "Grandpa, did they have computers when you were a kid?"

Grandpa thought for a moment.

"Yes, they did," he said. "After lunch we'll take Mr. Major for a walk, and I'll tell you about some computers that are very old indeed."

"So tell me about those very old computers," said Ollie as they walked through the woods.

"Well, believe it or not, computers existed even when I was a boy."

"What did they look like? Dad says computers used to be huge."

"Not all of them. The computers I'm thinking of were rather small. And if I remember correctly, there's one in my garden shed."

"A computer? In your shed? I don't believe you," said Ollie. "Did you make it yourself?"

Grandpa laughed. "No, it was made by someone much bigger."

Ollie looked up at his grandfather. He was six feet tall. Six foot one in his cap. Someone bigger than him? Amazing!

"I can even show you where
the computer was made."

"Huh? A computer factory here,
in Forest Hills?"

"Why not?" said Grandpa. "This
business has been in operation for
thousands of years."

"Grandpa, you're kidding, aren't you?"
said Ollie. He couldn't believe his
grandfather suddenly knew more about
computers than he did.

"No. It's the truth. I promise you!" said
Grandpa, and he looked as if he meant it.

On the other side of the river were
lots of little gardens. One of them was
Grandpa's.

"Is there really a computer in that shed?" asked Ollie. "Wouldn't it rust?"

"My computer is guaranteed not to
rust," said Grandpa cheerfully.

"I hope you remembered to bring the
key," said Ollie.

"No," said Grandpa. "I left it under the
flowerpot, as usual."

"Even though there's a *computer* in
there?"

"Uh-huh." Grandpa unlocked the door.

"That's crazy," said Ollie. "It could be stolen!" He walked inside and saw garden tools, a scarecrow, dusty old furniture, and spiders' webs. Could there really be a computer among all that junk?

Grandpa opened the shutters.

But even with sunlight flooding in, Ollie couldn't see a computer.

"Where *is* your computer, then? And how can it run without electricity—is it a portable with a battery?"

"Well, it is portable, but it runs on solar power," said Grandpa with a sly chuckle.

Ollie was impressed. Grandpa must be a technological wizard after all!

Grandpa was rummaging around, muttering, "Don't tell me a mouse has eaten it!"

Ollie looked at his grandfather suspiciously. Now he was really confused. How could a mouse eat a computer?

"Oh, well," said Grandpa. "I'll tell you the secret of my ancient computer outside."

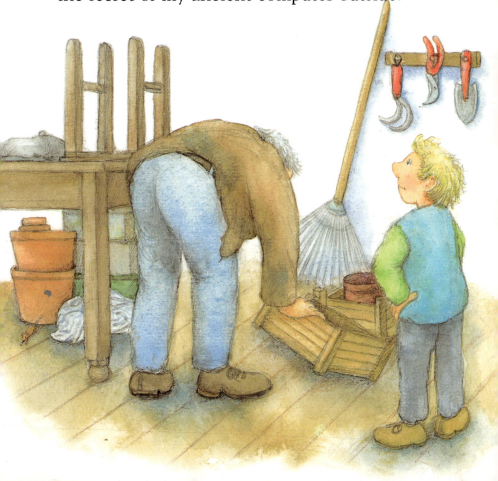

Mr. Major was watering one of the huge sunflowers that grew along the garden fence.

"Wow! They're even taller than you," said Ollie. He stood and stared at them.

"Much bigger than me," Grandpa agreed. He stooped to pick up something.

Ollie looked at him expectantly.

Grandpa said nothing for a while.

"The computer," Ollie reminded him. Grandpa certainly was getting forgetful!

"Yes, yes. I know. It's here in my hand," said Grandpa. "Come and sit down, and I'll show it to you."

Grandpa slowly opened his hand.

"Abracadabra! Here it is! It's a handy size, with smart black-and-white stripes, and streamlined, too!"

On the palm of Grandpa's hand lay a sunflower seed!

Ollie was really disappointed.

"You can't kid me," he said. "That's only a sunflower seed!"

"You're right," said Grandpa. "But you mustn't underestimate my sunflower-seed computer. It can run the most incredible program. You'd be amazed how much memory this little seed has."

"You mean it stores information, like a floppy disk?" asked Ollie.

Grandpa nodded. "This tiny seed holds the plans for making a whole plant: leaves, flowers, and all," he said.

"It knows how to take all it needs, from the air and the soil and the sunlight, to make the plant grow."

"And it knows how a stem should be constructed, so it can carry water all the way up to the flower head—without any kind of pump!"

Grandpa cut a sunflower.

"The stem is hollow," said Ollie.

"That's right," said Grandpa. "That makes it light and flexible, so it bends in the wind and doesn't break."

He held the heavy flower head in his hands.

In the middle were hundreds of seeds.

"It looks like a cake," said Ollie.
"And our little computer knows
exactly how long to bake this cake!"
said Grandpa.

"You could call it a computer cake," he went on. "Every summer, hundreds of little sunflower-seed computers ripen in each flower. And they can all make copies of themselves. No other computer can do that!"

"And next year, those hundreds of sunflowers can each make hundreds more," said Ollie. "And the year after that . . . Wow! You could take over the world with your sunflower-seed computers!"

"I could," said Grandpa, "if it weren't for the birds."

Grandpa threw the sunflower seed on
the ground.

A sparrow swooped down and ate it.

"There's another good thing about this computer," said Grandpa. "It can be recycled when you've finished with it. When most computers are out-of-date, no one wants them, not even the birds!"

Ollie was very quiet for a few minutes. He was thinking.

"Is it the same with all plants?" he asked after a while.

"More or less," said Grandpa. "Tulips have bulb computers. Daisy-seed computers are even smaller than this one. And cherries and peaches have pit computers."

Ollie pointed to the apple tree. "So inside every apple seed there's a program for making a great big apple tree?" he asked.

"There certainly is."

"Wow! That's amazing!"

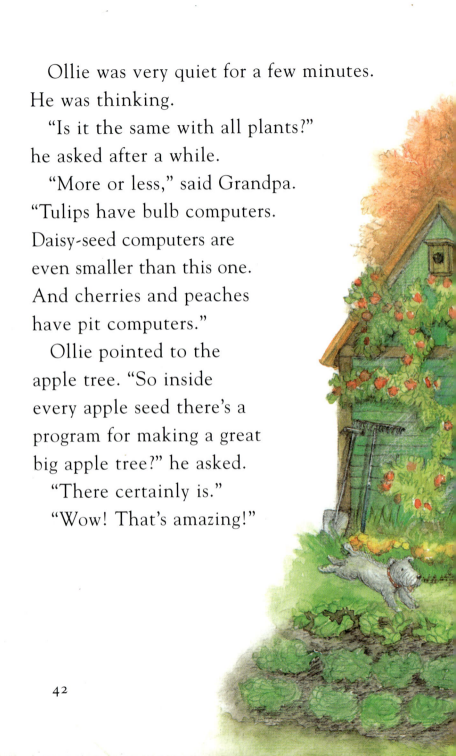

Ollie picked up an empty nutshell. He filled it with soil and pressed a sunflower seed into it.

"I'm going to take this home for Dad," he said. "I'll tell him it's a sunflower-seed computer in a nutshell!"

"Good idea," said Grandpa. "And ask him if any of his computers are as amazing as this one."

ABOUT THE AUTHOR

Ursel Scheffler was born in Nuremberg, a German city where many toys are made. She has written over one hundred children's books, which have been published in fifteen different languages. Her other easy-to-read books for North-South are *The Spy in the Attic* and a trio of adventures featuring a sly fox and a duck detective: *Rinaldo, the Sly Fox*; *The Return of Rinaldo, the Sly Fox*; and *Rinaldo on the Run*.

ABOUT THE ILLUSTRATOR

Ruth Scholte van Mast was born in Vreden, Germany. She drew a lot as a child, especially animals and children. She trained as a graphic artist, and drew printing patterns for wallpaper. Later she studied graphic design, and now works as a freelance children's book illustrator. This is her first book for North-South.

**Other Easy-to-Read books
by Ursel Scheffler:**

The Spy in the Attic
illustrated by Christa Unzner

•

Rinaldo, the Sly Fox
The Return of Rinaldo, the Sly Fox
Rinaldo on the Run
all illustrated by Iskender Gider